FAT CAMP COMMANDOS

By DANIEL PINKWATER

Illustrated by ANDY RASH

SCHOLASTIC PRESS/NEW YORK

Text copyright © 2001 by Daniel Pinkwater
Illustrations copyright © 2001 by Andy Rash

Library of Congress Cataloging-in-Publication Data

Pinkwater, Daniel Manus, 1941-
Fat camp commandos / by Daniel Pinkwater. – 1st ed.
p.   cm.
Summary: Ralph and Sylvia Nebula and their friend Mavis Goldfarb are
bitter at being sent to a bogus weight-loss camp, so they decide to
escape and find a way to take revenge on those responsible for
promoting the idea that thin is better.
ISBN 0-439-15527-4
[1. Overweight persons – Fiction.   2. Self-acceptance – Fiction.
3. Camps – Fiction.   4. Humorous stories.]
I. Rash, Andy, ill.   II. Title.

PZ7.P6335 Far 2001   [Fic] – dc21   00-058378

10 9 8 7 6 5 4 3 2 1   01 02 03 04 05

Printed in the U.S.A.   37
First Edition, May 2001
The text type was set in 15-point Coop Light.
Book design by Kristina Albertson

To my chubby cutie

Shredded carrots with raisins. Every meal at Camp Noo Yoo includes shredded carrots with raisins. Except breakfast. Breakfast is one puny pancake and sugar-free syrup that tastes like mouth-wash . . . and chopped orange salad with raisins. It's hot and steamy in the Camp

Noo Yoo dining room. Everything is served at room temperature, and the tables are always moist.

Yoo-hoo, Camp Noo Yoo! We love you!

We're Noo Yoo campers, true-blue-hoo!

We play some games, and lose
some pounds,

And sing some songs, and hang around.

Yoo-hoo, Camp Noo Yoo! We love you!

When we came we were lard-butts,

The diet was hard, but . . .

Yoo-hoo, Camp Noo Yoo! We love you!

Richard Tator is the owner of Camp Noo Yoo. During the school year he is a gym teacher. Some of the campers had him for gym - they hate him. During the school year, the kids have to call him Mr. Tator. At Camp Noo Yoo, he wants us to call him Dick. And we do - we call him Dick Tator. He wears his whistle in the shower and when he sleeps.

Mountainburg is where the fortune-telling chickens come from. In cheap arcades and bus stations throughout the South, and creepy bars and gas stations, people have these fortune-telling chick-

ens in wire cages. You drop a coin in a
slot, a bell rings, and the chicken drops a
little rolled-up piece of paper down a little slide. . . . It's got your fortune printed
on it. Mountainburg is where these chickens – as well as dancing chickens, piano-
playing chickens, and opera-singing
chickens – are bred and trained by Dick
Tator's father, who is known as Pa Tator.

Besides Pa Tator's chicken farm, there's a little store, which is also a lunch counter, a newsstand, and the bus stop. The chicken farm is right next to Camp Noo Yoo.

Dick Tator's twin younger brothers, Bud and Spud, run the store. They are evil and corrupt - which is a good thing for the Noo Yoo campers. Bud and Spud deliver pizza and french fries and candy bars to the campers after dark. During the day, they lounge around the store/lunch counter/newsstand/bus stop, along with a couple of their favorite attack-trained chickens. Bud and Spud, the punky brothers - and their punky chickens - are the first ones you see when you arrive in Mountainburg by bus, and the last ones you see when you leave.

VI.

Noo Yoo is a fat camp. The campers wear three layers of sweatsuits when they play softball, to sweat off those pounds. There are compulsory aerobics three times a day. There are Creative Abuse and Motivation classes three nights a week. There are special diet meals – (remember the shredded carrots and raisins?). The idea is that Mommy and Daddy's pudgy darling goes off to camp a little butterball, and comes back a fashion model. This has never happened once, but people send their kids anyway.

#

I am Ralph Nebula. My sister, Sylvia, is another Noo Yoo camper. It all started on Anti-Fat Day in Pokooksie, New York, our hometown. Anti-Fat Day is a local holiday in Pokooksie.

#

Anti-Fat Day in Pokooksie is nearly as big as Halloween. The regular citizens all try to get the fat citizens to go on diets and become thin citizens. They do this because thin is better, and they love their fat fellow-citizens. They express this love by having a fat-parade. They will pelt you with cream-filled doughnuts if

8

you're fat, and call you names. This is because they love you. It strikes me as
strange that most of the so-called thin
citizens of Pokooksie are not all that thin.
I'd say the average Pokooksian is above
average when it comes to weight. The average Pokooksian is below average in
most other respects.

IX.

Anti-Fat Day was started by a Dr.
Frizzbender and Dick Tator (who else?).
Dick Tator hired kids to pass out fact
sheets about Camp Noo Yoo, and my
mother got one. The next thing I knew, my
mother and father and sister Sylvia and I
were in the community room of the
Pokooksie Motel, listening to Dick Tator

talk about the camp. And there was a special speaker, Dick Tator's personal hero, Simon Primly. Simon Primly is a famous weight-loss guy. He goes around and finds people who have gotten so fat they can't get out the door, and he prays with them, and sings to them, and hugs them, and feeds them shredded carrots, until they are all skinny and perfect, and then he shows them off. Simon Primly gave a speech.

"People! You are SO fortunate to have a man like Dick Tator in your community. I mean SO fortunate! Because Dick Tator cares about you! Dick Tator loves you! Dick Tator especially cares about your

unhappy, fat little children! Looking
around the room, I see so many round,
fat, unhappy children. They are going to
grow up miserable. They will be hated.
They will become stupid. And many of
them will turn to crime. Why? Because
that is what happens to fat people. I don't
want your children to be fat stupid crimi-
nals, hated by everyone. Look! I'm crying,
I'm so sincere! Sign your kids up for
Camp Noo Yoo. Even if you can't afford
it – you have to do this – it's . . . for . . .
the . . . children."

XI.

This is Ralph speaking again. Simon
Primly got so worked up that he had to
wipe his nose with the hem of his athletic

shirt, which gave the crowd a look at his hairy tummy – which was a little fat. I thought he was a raving maniac. I am fat, and so is my sister, Sylvia, also our mother and father. None of us are stupid. Nobody hates us. And I never thought about turning to crime until Simon Primly mentioned it.

XII.

My mother was crying. My father was crying. Sylvia and I were crying, too, but for different reasons.

"How could we let this happen?" my mother blubbered. "Our children are fat!"

"I know! I know!" my father wailed.

"This is silly," I said. "You are fat yourselves. It's the way we are."

"We have to save them! We have to sign them up for Camp Noo Yoo!"

There was no reasoning with them. That Simon Primly is very motivational.

Forward in time: The peaceful little hamlet of Mountainburg. The Noo Yoo campers are tucked in their beds, dreaming of fried dough. All is quiet except for the faint sound of chickens practicing on electric keyboards. In the farmhouse right next to the camp, Ma Tator is serving fried chicken to her husband Pa, and their boys, Dick, Bud, and Spud. Besides the fried chicken, there are mashed potatoes with butter, mashed turnips with butter, mashed squash with butter, corn on the cob with butter and salt and pepper, creamed spinach with butter, dumplings, fritters, biscuits, rolls, apple pie, cherry pie, rhubarb pie, blueberry pie, and cups of coffee - with butter. The good smells of the kitchen waft through the cabins and cause the campers to twitch in their sleep.

While Mountainburg sleeps, the Camp Noo Yoo counselors, all of whom have completed two years of high school before dropping out, are in the Camp Noo Yoo bus. They're headed for a club in Yonkers, New York, where there is a band that uses rusty razor blades as guitar picks, and the members of the audience hit themselves on the head

with hammers instead of clapping their
hands.

#

This is Ralph again. Who was that, talking just now?

XVI.

There was a camper had a snack,

And Pickle was its name-O!

P-I-C-K-L-E,

P-I-C-K-L-E,

P-I-C-K-L-E,

And Pickle was its name-O!

It hardly has a calorie,

And Pickle is its name-O!

C-A-L-O-R-I-E,

C-A-L-O-R-I-E,

C-A-L-O-R-I-E,

And Pickle is its name-O!

XVII.

Creative Abuse and Motivation. This activity turned out to be a mixed bag including Simon Primly videos, campers getting weighed in front of everybody by Ma Tator, the camp nurse, and lectures by Dick Tator. The lectures went like this:

"Here's what you have to look forward to as a fat adult: You live alone in a nasty little room because no one will marry a big fat tub like you. The room is nasty because you can't afford anything nice, because you can't get a decent job . . . because you're fat! People laugh at you in the street, insult you, and throw doughnuts at you. You lose your job collecting dead skunks for the Fish and Wildlife Service, because you're too fat. You wind up in prison for stealing pumpkin pies

from the postdated pie store the day after Thanksgiving."

At first, these sessions were fun, while
Dick Tator was putting his whole heart in
it, but soon he started repeating himself,
and all the enjoyment went out of it.

XVIII.

Camp Noo Yoo has many features in
addition to the weight-loss and reeduca-
tion programs. Beautiful Lake Nish-du-
ge-dak has mostly dried up, but it still
offers pleasing views and remains the
center of campus life. The Noo Yoo
woods have been cut down for lumber,
but the underbrush remains a source of
nature study . . . especially rich in poi-
sonous snakes, to delight the budding

herpetologist. Crafts available include a roof-repair workshop, and classes in traditional stone-wall building. A modern swimming pool is under construction and should be finished next year.

XIX.

Sylvia's cabin was called "Olive Oyl." Mine was "Mahatma Gandhi." Neither of us saw our counselor after the second day. It seems they never came back from their road trip to the rock club in Yonkers. Dick Tator came by and told the kids in both cabins that he would get us new counselors soon. He didn't, of course. We didn't see that it made much difference. The kids whose cabins still had counselors told us that they spent most of their time visiting the coun-selors at Camp No-Tubs-We, another diet camp on the other side of Lake Nish-du-ge-dak. You couldn't walk directly across Lake Nish-du-ge-dak (even though it only had a couple of inches of water) because of the quicksand. A kid could sink out of sight in a minute. So the counselors had

to walk all the way around the edge of
the lake. We could hear them laughing and
singing late at night.

The other kids at Noo Yoo were all
more or less overweight like Sylvia and
me, but they didn't seem to be as mad as
we were. Maybe it was because our parents had never done anything like this to
us before. Most of the other kids had
been sent to fat-doctors, and fat-
classes, and other fat-camps before this.
They were able to accept it. We weren't.

XXI.

As far as I could tell, there was only one cool kid at Camp Noo Yoo. It was Mavis Goldfarb, the A-plus student and Celtic witch. She lived in the counselor-less Olive Oyl cabin with my sister. Mavis hated Noo Yoo, hated Dick Tator, and hated her parents for being dumb enough to send her there. Mavis was a little, round fatball of fury.

XXII.

Mavis, Sylvia, and I were in the nature cabin, polishing off our nightly mushroom and pepperoni pizza, delivered by Bud and Spud, the younger brothers of Dick Tator. It was quiet in the nature cabin, and we weren't bothered by kids wanting to share our pizza. There were a dozen or fifteen rattlesnakes in wire cages. They'd been picked up hanging around the cabins, and were scheduled to be cooked for the campers. They say the meat tastes just like chicken, and it's low calorie. The skins were going to the crafts cabin so we could make belts - two inches too small - to motivate us.

XXIII.

"What do you say we give these ser-
pents their freedom?" I asked. The snakes
were being quiet - no rattling. I think they
were glad to have some company.

"What do you say we give *ourselves*
our freedom?" Mavis Goldfarb, the Celtic
witch, asked.

"What? You mean escape? Disappear?
Blow this pop stand?" Sylvia asked.

"That's what I mean," Mavis said.

"Cool," Sylvia said. "How do we do it?"

XXIV.

"You came here on the bus from
Pokooksie, right?" Mavis asked. "Well, Dick
Tator saved three bucks by buying each

of us a round-trip ticket. The return tickets are in our folders in the camp office - and the folders are in the file cabinet, which isn't locked."

"We steal our tickets?"

"What steal? They're our tickets. They have our names on them."

"And then we just go?" I asked. "What happens when someone tells on us?"

"Who's going to tell?" Mavis asked. "Our counselors? We don't have any. The other kids in our cabins? We'll ask them not to mention it. It's simple. It's foolproof."

"What about Bud and Spud?" Sylvia asked. "They'll see us at the bus station."

"Five dollars apiece will buy their silence," Mavis said.

"Wow. So we can just go?"

"We can be eating better pizza in Pokooksie tomorrow night," Mavis said.

"Okay. I'm sold," I said. "Help me turn these snakes loose in Dick Tator's front yard, and we're on our way."

XXV.

If you're chubby and you know it

Clap your hands!

If you're chubby and you know it

Clap your hands!

If you're a fatso and you know it

And your tubby tummy shows it

If you're chubby and you know it

Clap your hands!

XXVI.

We sang quietly, under our breaths, as the fourteen satisfyingly fat rattlers slithered under Dick Tator's front porch. Then we went to pry open the door to the office.

XXVII.

The next morning, we were on the Pokooksie bus, and two hours from home. It had gone just as Mavis said it would. We had dragged our duffel bags, with our bus tickets in them, out the front gate of Camp Noo Yoo just as the sun came up. They were already yelling and carrying on at Dick Tator's house.

"There's another one!" we heard Pa
Tator holler. "It's eating my Rice Krispies!"

"Get a broom! Get a broom!" Ma Tator
was screaming.

It was good to leave Camp Noo Yoo on
a high note. This way, we'd have happy
memories of our farewell to Mountainburg.

XXVIII.

"My sister tells me you're a witch," I said to Mavis.

"That's right, bub."

"I don't think I ever met a witch before," I said. "What's involved, exactly?"

"Various things," Mavis Goldfarb answered. "Most important is, don't get me mad at you."

"I'll keep it in mind."

"Do that."

XXIX.

"HOW long before they come for us, do you think?" Sylvia asked. "You suppose we'll have a whole day before we're busted?"

"What are you talking about?" Mavis Goldfarb asked. "They're never going to bust us. We're getting away with this completely."

"How do you figure that?" I asked.

"Well, the kids at Noo Yoo have enough to think about, just trying to get hold of black-market pizza and avoiding rattle-snakes. They're going to forget all about us. Since we had no counselors, we won't be reported missing. We left everything nice and neat in the office, so no one knows our bus tickets are gone. Dick Tator won't miss us until the end of camp, when he looks in our folders.

I unwrapped a candy bar - we'd stocked up at the Mountainburg store.

"And then Dick Tator calls our parents and we're busted. By the way, where have we been between now and the end of camp? We don't have much money or anyplace to hide out. I don't see us lasting on the street a whole twenty-four hours."

"Give me some credit," Mavis Goldfarb said. "On the last day of camp, you two just turn up at your house, smiling and happy. When Dick Tator calls to say he doesn't know where you are, he'll look like an idiot. As to where you'll stay - you're coming to my house. My parents are in Africa, looking for fossils. We'll have the place to ourselves. I think you'll be comfortable."

XXXI.

Right in the middle of Pokooksie, New York, there is a ten-foot-tall fence. It's a chain-link fence. It goes on for about a block, then it turns a corner, and goes on for another block. Then it turns a corner, runs another block, and turns the last corner and completes a square. On the inside, there are thick bushes up against the fence, so you can't see through. There is a gate in the fence, which is always closed, and a few feet in from the gate is a tall, thick hedge, which makes it impossible to see anything inside the fenced area.

No one knows what's inside the fence. Some people say there was a big mansion there a hundred years ago, but it burned down, and the grounds grew wild. Some people say it's a private zoo. Some people say a mad scientist lives there. Some say a zillionaire. But nobody knows.

I know. My sister Sylvia knows. Inside the block-square, ten-foot-high, hedge-backed, chain-link fence is Mavis Goldfarb's house.

XXXII.

Mavis Goldfarb's house is large and tall, made of wood, with lots of pointy arches, and wooden knobs and spires, and curly things. There's a wide porch all around it, and canvas awnings over the windows. It looked like an old picture in the mid-morning light.

"Plenty of room here, as you can see," Mavis Goldfarb said.

"Will it be okay for us to just stay

here? I mean without permission from any adults or anything?" Sylvia asked.

"Well, if it will make you feel any better, we can get permission from an adult," Mavis said. "Here comes old Shlermie, the gardener. Hey, Shlermie! Is it all right with you if these kids stay here for a while?"

A man wearing a black suit and tie and gardening gloves, who was pushing a wheelbarrow, had appeared from behind the house. "Miss Mavis!" he said. "Are you back from camp already? Would your friends like to freshen up before breakfast? I will prepare something for you all."

"Old Shlermie is like one of the family," Mavis said.

XXXIII.

The inside of the house was nice – quiet and comfortable. All the windows were open, and a cool breeze blew through the place. Sylvia and I were shown to little bedrooms that looked out at the gardens old Shlermie took care of.

I could smell bacon frying and toast toasting – and I could hear plates and silverware clinking. Old Shlermie was fixing breakfast. I was already in love with Mavis Goldfarb's house, and I'd only been in it for fifteen minutes.

XXXIV.

"So, didn't it sort of kill you to have to leave someplace as beautiful as this, and go to Camp Noo Yoo?" I asked Mavis Goldfarb, after my second helping of bacon and eggs.

"It made me wild," Mavis Goldfarb said. "They pushed me into it. My protests and my rational arguments were ignored, and do you know why?"

"Why?" we asked.

"Because they panicked! They were terrified! They allowed an idiot like Dick Tator to sell them something that was obviously no good. They would never have bought a new refrigerator based on such crummy arguments – but they were willing to send their only daughter's actual body to that bogus camp."

"Our parents, too," Sylvia said. "And they never bugged us about being fat before. They're fat themselves. What made them go simple in the head like that?"

XXXV.

"**Look,**" Mavis Goldfarb said. "One in five kids in America is overweight, and one in TWO adults is. The scientists are still trying to work out exactly why this is so - they don't have a clue of what to do about it."

"Everybody goes on a diet?" I asked.

"Except diets don't work," Mavis said. "Practically nobody loses weight on one, and practically all those who do gain it back. The odds are more than ninety-nine to one that if you are fat now, you're going to be fat later."

"How do you know all this?" I asked Mavis Goldfarb.

"I read books, bub."

"So . . . what are you saying? We're doomed to be fat?" Sylvia asked.

"There is fat, and then there is fat,"

Mavis said. "I can do a hundred push-ups and then beat you at tennis. I don't call it doomed. I call it the way I am."

XXXVI.

"**Will** you be taking revenge on your parents for sending you to that camp, Miss Mavis?" old Shlermie asked.

"You know me well, Shlermie," Mavis Goldfarb said. "But they are digging up fossils in Olduvai Gorge. I was thinking of taking revenge on society in general."

"Very good, Miss Mavis," old Shlermie said. "And will your little friends be joining you in terrorizing ordinary citizens to awaken them from their fat-prejudice?"

Mavis Goldfarb looked at us. "What do you say? Do you want to help me give a

mental hotfoot to the people of Pokooksie?"

Sylvia and I looked at each other. "We *are* pretty cheesed-off at our parents for letting Dick Tator talk them into sending us to that living hell."

"They will be among the victims," Mavis said.

"We're not going to kill anybody?" I asked.

"No. Nothing like that. This is psycho-
logical war," Mavis said.

"Count us in!" Sylvia and I said.

XXXVII.

We started small. That very day, we
went to the Burns and Numble Giant
Bookstore and visited the diet book sec-
tion. We also visited the dessert cook-
book section. We sort of mixed them
together, so it went: *The Last Diet Book
You Will Ever Need,* and next to it
*Secrets of Swiss Chocolate Cakes and
Pies,* and then *The Very Last Diet Book
You Will Ever Need,* which was shelved
beside *One Thousand and One Cookie
Recipes.* After that *This Is Really, Really,
Really the Last Diet Book You Will Ever
Need,* and then *The Illustrated*

Encyclopedia of French Pastry (Mavis Goldfarb has that one at home). On the same shelf was *I Swear to God, This Is the Last Diet Book You Will Ever, Ever Need, I Promise*, and cuddled up against it was *Creampuffs and Éclairs Made Simple*.

Bookstores can be educational. We learned that if you read the titles of diet books, one after another, you realize they are stupid and couldn't possibly work - otherwise why would there be so many of them? Burns and Numble has hundreds. We also learned that dessert cookbooks have beautiful photography. I wonder if there are special food photographers - I wouldn't mind being one.

XXXVIII.

Burns and Numble has a little coffee area right inside the bookstore. We got cups of mint tea and slices of double chocolate cake. It was very nice sipping tea and nibbling cake in the big bookstore. They have good air-conditioning, and classical music plays on the sound system. People can bring books to the tables and read while they snack.

A skinny woman wearing jogging shorts and a top that showed her stringy neck and ropy arm muscles was sitting at a table nearby, staring at us. She looked angry. Finally, she came over to us and said, "Look at you! You children are overweight! And you're eating cake! Don't you have any self-control? Don't you have any self-respect? How can you let yourselves get that way? How can your parents let you sit around and eat cake?" She was pretty upset. The veins in her neck were jumping and twitching.

Mavis Goldfarb spoke. "Lady . . . you are suffering from a form of insanity. Go away . . . or my friends and I will be forced to eat you."

The lady went away to find the manager and report us for threatening cannibalism.

"You see?" Mavis Goldfarb asked. "This is what we're up against. People are irrational. Ours is an important mission."

#

The next day we thought we'd take a cue from the crazy lady in the bookstore, and confront some people directly. Something Mavis, Sylvia, and I have in

common – besides being fat and tired of being pushed around – is that we are good runners. We enjoy jogging. I'm not saying we're Olympic material, but we can keep up with most people, including most adults. When we went out for our morning trot, we gave our own version of Creative Abuse and Motivation to runners we met.

"Hey, look at her!" Mavis said, as we

overtook a girl with not an ounce of fat on her. "What's her name? Beanpole?"

"You shouldn't run at your weight," Sylvia said as we thundered past her. "You should rest a lot and eat nourishing food."

This was cruel. I was enjoying it.

"Hey, pipe-cleaner man! Get out of the way! If we bump into you, you'll get bent."

As we ran along insulting people, I was realizing that this sort of thing had been done to me all my life – and I had sort of pushed it down and never thought about it.

"Beep-beep, Skinny! You'd be able to pick up those feet better if you ate something besides bean sprouts!"

We had a good run and got back to Mavis's house feeling happy and ready for a good breakfast.

XL.

"**I feel** a little bad about saying all those mean things," Sylvia said.

"And yet, at the same time . . . ?" Mavis said.

"And yet, at the same time, I wonder if anybody ever felt bad about saying similar things to me."

"Bingo!" Mavis said. "People in general think if you're fat, they can say whatever they like. The people we told off today now might think twice about insulting someone who looks a little different."

"Remember that lady in the bookstore," I said. "She thought she had a right to lecture us, just because she's skinny and thinks that's neat - and we're not."

"And we don't think it's particularly neat," Mavis said. "Now, put on something with horizontal stripes, kids. We're going to a Junior Weight Whippers meeting."

XLI.

"**Junior** Weight Whippers? Isn't that one of those weight-losing clubs?" I asked.

"They call it a club, but it's a for-profit business." Mavis said. "However, today is free. It's a special offer to rope in new fatties. Let's see if they can help us."

At the Weight Whippers Center, there were a bunch of miserable-looking, de-pressed kids. Most of them were heavy - some weren't at all, but appar-ently thought they were.

We all took seats in an auditorium, and a perky lady, whose name was Judi, told us all about the Junior Weight Whippers program. She told us if we came to meetings (and our parents paid), we'd lose weight, and it would be easy, and then we'd be popular.

Then she told us how our lives would stink if we stayed fat, and we'd probably all wind up killing ourselves because we didn't look like her. We'd heard it all before from Dick Tator.

Mavis raised her hand. "Judi, does the Junior Weight Whippers diet really work?"

"Of course it works, honey," Judi said.

"Does everybody get thin?" Mavis asked.

"Everybody who comes to meetings gets thin!" Judi said.

"But I did research on the Internet," Mavis said. "I downloaded statistics from a hundred serious medical websites. All the figures I found said that less than

one person in a thousand loses weight,
and, of those, less than one in a thousand keeps it off for two years, which is
the longest study anyone has ever done."

"Those figures are wrong, little girl,"
Judi said. "Save your questions for later.
We will now tell you more about the
yummy Junior Weight Whippers diet."

XLII.

"Are we allowed to have cheeseburg-
ers on the Junior Weight Whippers diet?"
Mavis asked.

"Yes, you are!" Judi said. "You can have
the special frozen Weight Whippers mini-
burger with cheese, which your mother
can buy in the frozen food section!"

"A frozen cheeseburger? Yich!" Mavis
said. "I wouldn't give that to a starving

dog in an alley. I'm talking about a real cheeseburger!"

Sylvia spoke up. "You mean like they have at Cheesy-Beefy just down the street?"

"Yes! That's a good cheeseburger! They use choice ground sirloin, and it's charcoal broiled to perfection. A slice of real cheddar cheese is partially melted on top, and the fresh-baked sesame-seed bun is lightly toasted. You can have it with nothing but a dollop of catsup, or California-style with tomatoes, onions, lettuce, and crisp dill pickle slices."

I stood up. "I like mine with grilled onions and catsup," I said, "and a pickle slice on the side. I also love their french fries, made from thick-cut king-size Idaho potatoes, fried crispy-crunchy in fresh peanut oil. The peanut oil is one of the secrets of the Cheesy-Beefy, did you know that?"

Even Judi was drooling. The meeting sort of broke up early. We saw Judi and a lot of the kids at Cheesy-Beefy, where we stopped for lunch.

"Fight on, Junior Weight Whippers," we said with fists raised in the Weight Whippers salute. "Shed those pounds and become popular – and try the cheese fries . . . they're yummy."

XLIII.

Being an outlaw and a fat-revolutionary felt good. Once we got started, it would have been hard to stop. But why stop? There were opportunities everywhere.

"Hello? Is this the Miracle Quick-Slim Company? You have an ad that says 'Lose three to eleven inches in one hour, doing the Miracle Quick-Slim program.'

Well, my brother has been doing the exercise for three hours, and now we can't find him."

XLIV.

Life was good, staying with Mavis Goldfarb. Old Shlermie, the gardener and man-of-all-work, whipped up very good meals, the house was comfortable and pleasant – and there were always things to do.

We went down to Bert's Shirts, the custom T-shirt while-you-wait place, and had T-shirts printed that said FAT PEOPLE ARE HAPPIER across the shoulders.

And we were.

XLV.

We went to King of Copies/Prince of Printing and had red-and-white stickers made. They were about the size of a playing card and read IF YOU'RE TEN POUNDS OR MORE OVERWEIGHT. The idea was that we'd add our stickers to signs in the mall that

said things like 10% OFF. If a shopper wanted the discount, he or she would have to announce they were fat. "Just to get them used to saying it," Mavis said.

"We're bad," Sylvia said. "We're fat and we're bad."

XLVI.

"**Let's** do something big," Mavis said one day. "I sent old Shlermie to the library to do research, and he found something pretty good."

"What's that?" Sylvia and I asked old Shlermie.

"Doctor Frizzbender, the local fat-quack, has a brother," Shlermie said, smiling brightly.

"So? Lot's of people have brothers. Why is that so good?"

"His brother is fat," Shlermie said, dancing on the tips of his toes.

"Oh, that *is* good! The anti-fat doctor's own brother is a fattie."

"It's even better," Shlermie said, hopping up and down. "You've seen Frizzbender's ads in the paper and on TV, where he shows the before-and-after pictures of himself as a fat guy and as the thin guy he is now?"

"Right! He went from fat to thin using his own method!"

"Only he didn't!" Shlermie shouted. "The 'before' picture is of his brother, Hugo, who lives about twenty miles away in Blue Hook, New York."

All of us were jumping up and down now.

"And Hugo hates his brother for being a big fake!" Mavis said.

"And! And! And-and-and! Frizzbender is going to be on the radio today!" Shlermie shouted.

"No!"

"Yes!"

"And-and-and-and it's a call-in show!"

"No!"

"Yes!"

"AND . . . We're going to call in . . . from Hugo's house!"

"Yaaaay!"

"Shlermie, fire up the Nash Rambler! We're going on a trip to Blue Hook!"

XLVII.

We had a nice ride to Blue Hook in the old Nash Rambler car. Shlermie wore white gloves when he drove it. He had prepared a picnic basket with fried chicken, cucumber salad, blueberry muffins, lemonade, and a lot of other stuff to take to Hugo Frizzbender.

Hugo Frizzbender lived in an old farm-house with vines growing on it. There was a big shady front porch, and that is where we had our picnic. Hugo was a nice guy. He wore overalls and had puffy white whiskers.

"My brother, Roger, is a complete wie-

nie," Hugo said. "He needs a public spank-
ing, so let's give him one."

Hugo had brought his radio out on the
porch, and we tuned in the Larry Who
show from Pokooksie.

"Today, we have a guest, Doctor Roger
Frizzbender, who claims to have helped
many people lose weight," Larry Who
said.

"Not just claimed, Larry," Dr.
Frizzbender said. "Have. Have helped.
Thousands."

"We're going to open the phone lines,"
Larry Who said. "Ask Doctor Frizzbender
your questions."

Sylvia was the first caller. "Dr.
Frizzbender, I am a fat little girl. My name
is Hortense."

"I can help you, Hortense," Dr.
Frizzbender said.

"I saw an ad you put in the *Pokooksie
Journal*," Sylvia said. "There was a big fat

man, and there was a thin man. Were they both you?"

"Yes, Hortense. I was that big fat man. I was my own first patient. I helped myself, and now I help others. If I can do it, you can do it."

XLVIII.

"**Hold** on a second, Doctor Frizzbender," Sylvia said. "I want to put someone else on the phone."

Hugo picked up the receiver. "Roger, you awful liar, this is your fat brother, Hugo. It is my picture in your phony advertisement. You were always a beanpole, and I've always been fat. You need to apologize to all the fat people you've swindled, taking their money and getting no results."

Dr. Frizzbender was sputtering. "Larry, this man is a fraud. I have no brother Hugo. Hang up on him."

"Is this true? Are you a fraud?" Larry Who asked.

"I am an attorney-at-law, licensed to practice in the state of New York, and everything I say is true," Hugo said. "There will be an item in the *Pokooksie Journal* tomorrow, with all the information."

"Well, I guess *you're* not a fraud," Larry Who said to Hugo.

"In the interest of full disclosure, Larry, we should tell your listeners that you and I have been friends since the third grade," Hugo said.

"That we have," Larry Who said, "and you are a fine gentleman."

"Thank you, Larry. Roger, find something honest to do. Good-bye, all," Hugo said, and put down the receiver.

We all hugged Hugo before we left, and promised to visit him again.

XLIX.

Every couple of days, Sylvia and I went to our own house while our parents were at work, did laundry, played with the dog, and dropped off a bogus letter from Camp Noo Yoo. These letters had beautiful Mountainburg postmarks, done in pencil by old Shlermie, who was a real artist.

Our fat parents had sworn that they

were going to diet at home while we were reduced at Camp Noo Yoo. This was to show solidarity with us, their children, and because they believed in the Dick Tator/Roger Frizzbender philosophy.

We checked the refrigerator each time we came, and while they weren't eating as well as we were at Mavis Goldfarb's house, they were certainly not eating badly.

Apparently, they were only gullible when it came to us. They were smart enough to figure out that the diet was intolerable . . . for them. Meanwhile, they believed we were eating shredded carrots at Noo Yoo. We had to punish them. So we shrank their underwear. We shrank all of it, every time we came over. Pretty soon, they bought new underwear, and we shrank that, too. It was satisfying to see they had gone to larger sizes.

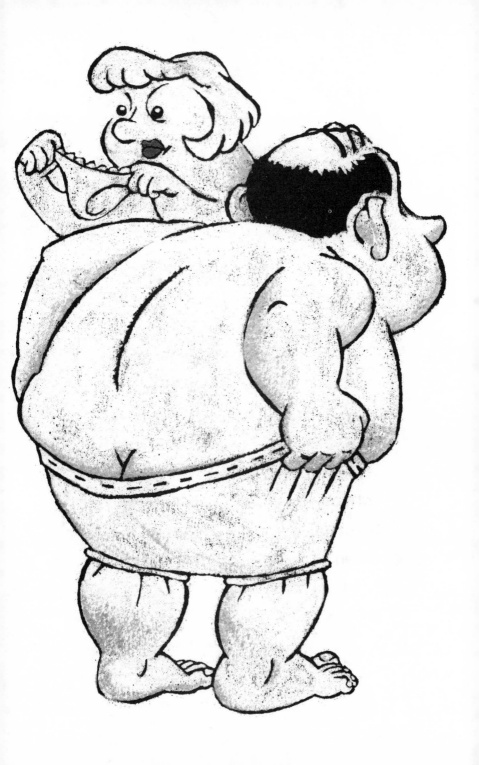

L.

Using duct tape and flexible dryer exhaust hose, we fed the exhaust fumes from Cinnamon Bunz Bakery into The Slim Gym.

Somehow, Shlermie got hold of a photo of Dick Tator wearing a Belly Binder corset with straps and laces, which squeezed his stomach and butt in and made him look thinner, but slightly lumpy. We made plenty of copies at King of Copies/Prince of Printing, and stored them away for the next Anti-Fat Day.

The summer was passing too quickly. But we were building golden memories.

LI.

Then, two unexpected things happened. The first unexpected thing happened when we went to the Moskowitz Cultural Center to heckle a speaker. The speaker's name was Dr. Deepdip Cha-cha, and his topic was "Fitness and Fatness – Which is Better?" It sounded like the usual garbage, and we brought bags of stale doughnuts to throw at him.

But, here's the unexpected thing, he made sense. Right from the beginning, he was reasonable.

"Look," Dr. Deepdip Cha-cha said. "Close to a third of our citizens are overweight – meaning heavier than the average person used to be. The media will tell you this is a bad thing – but we don't really know. Doctors know hardly anything about fat and thin.

"One thing we do know is that none . . . that is, NONE . . . of the known methods of weightloss are very effective. And some may be dangerous.

"So, try to lose some weight, if you want to, but don't do anything extreme. Don't do crazy diets with eating only one or two things. Don't starve yourself. Getting some extra exercise is probably the best thing you can do – but don't overdo that either. Be nice to your body, and you will have a nice body.

"And most important, don't get tricked into hating the way you look. The people who tell you that you have to be thin to be a happy person are either idiots, or they're trying to sell you something that isn't going to work anyway."

"Wow, this guy makes sense," Mavis said.

"And he's even a doctor," I said. "They're usually crazy."

LII.

We walked slowly, going back to Mavis Goldfarb's house after Deepdip Cha-cha's lecture. We were thoughtful.

"You know," Sylvia said. "That Deepdip guy is talking about the same things we are."

"He is," I said. "Only he's . . . constructive. He doesn't go around trashing people and things to make his point."

"That's true," Mavis said. "But he's some kind of doctor with lots of education, and people respect him and go to hear him speak."

"Whereas, we are merely children, and our voices tend to be unheard," I said.

"So, we will continue to trash things?" Sylvia asked.

"Of course," Mavis said.

"They were selling Deepdip Cha-cha

cassettes in the lobby. Did you notice?" I asked.

"So he isn't perfect," Mavis said. "Cut the man some slack. You don't want to turn into a fanatic."

The second unexpected thing happened when we were coming down from the billboard on Ninth Street. We had just added about forty pounds to the girl in the swimsuit advertisement for Pokooksie Sausage Products.

We were standing and admiring her, holding the paint can and the ladder, when a voice said, "Hello, hello, hello! What's all this, then?"

LIV.

We were busted. A big fat cop was towering over us.

"What you just did . . . improving the swimsuit of the model on the billboard . . . is called, 'defacing private property,' and it's against the law," the cop said.

"It's a protest," Mavis Goldfarb said. "It's a protest against images that create prejudice against unpopular body types. Did you know that kids our age go on dangerous starvation diets because they are afraid society will reject them unless they are way too skinny?"

"I knew that," the cop said.

"Did you know that billions of dollars are wasted every year on diet books, diet foods, diet pills, and other diet products, not one of which has been proven to work?"

"I knew that, too," the cop said. "By the way, I'm Officer A. John Pup."

"Mavis Goldfarb," Mavis said. "Pleased to meet you, Officer Pup. These are my friends, Sylvia and Ralph Nebula."

We shook hands with Officer Pup.

"Did you know," Officer Pup said, "that people guilty of defacing property are subject to fine and/or imprisonment, and

may be asked to pay to restore the property they defaced?"

"No, we didn't know that," we said.

"Are we going to jail?" Sylvia asked.

"The usual procedure would be to take you to the station house, fingerprint you, take your photos, and call your parents. We might keep you in jail for a few hours. And then later, you come before a judge."

"Oh, noooo," we moaned.

"However, the officer at the scene can decide whether a warning or some other measure will be enough."

"And? Is a warning enough?" Mavis asked.

"Well, you didn't actually ruin the bill-board. You just made the model look . . . rounder. You did a very good job, in my opinion," Officer Pup said.

"We were careful," Mavis said.

"We're basically good children," I said.

"Don't push your luck," Officer Pup

said. "As I was about to say, I could warn you. I could make you promise to stop doing things like this. I won't ask you what else you've done, but I have my suspicions. Are you willing to promise?"

"What happens if we don't promise?" Mavis asked.

"I take you in," Officer Pup said.

"We promise," we all said at once.

"There is one more thing," Officer Pup said.

"Yes?"

"You have to show up at the Moskowitz Cultural Center at 7:00 P.M. tomorrow night. Fail to be there, and I will hunt you down like dogs."

"What happens at the Moskowitz

Cultural Center at 7:00 P.M. tomorrow night?"

Officer Pup smiled, twirled the ends of his moustache, turned and walked away, with his hands clasped behind his back, singing.

My object all sublime

I shall achieve in time –

To let the punishment fit the crime –

The punishment fit the crime;

And make each prisoner pent

Unwillingly represent

A source of innocent merriment!

Of innocent merriment!

LVII.

The next night, at 7:00 P.M., Mavis
Goldfarb, my sister, Sylvia Nebula, and I,
Ralph Nebula, found ourselves at the
Moskowitz Cultural Center at a meeting of
the Pokooksie Overweight Gilbert and
Sullivan Society.

Gilbert and Sullivan, I already knew,
but had to explain to Mavis and Sylvia,
were these English guys who wrote
operettas – or little operas or musical
comedies – at the end of the nineteenth
century. They were really popular, and
still are, sort of.

The Pokooksie Overweight Gilbert and
Sullivan Society is a large group of large
people, who put on Gilbert and Sullivan
operettas for their own amusement.
Actually, you don't have to be a large
person to be a member, but when they

put on the show, thin people have to wear fat-costumes, so everyone on stage looks round.

We had no idea anything like this went on in Pokooksie.

We had no idea there were so many fat people.

We had no idea they got together and put on shows.

Sylvia and Mavis had no idea who Gilbert and Sullivan were.

And I had no idea what the music sounded like – which was pretty good, actually. Some of the members of the Overweight Gilbert and Sullivan Society had decent voices.

LVIII.

Officer Pup was there. He was playing a police sergeant, and the name of the operetta was *The Pirates of Penzance*.

"Ah, there you all are!" Officer Pup said to us. "It's all arranged. You're going to be pirates in the chorus. I hope you can all sing good and loud . . . or anyway loud."

"And if we don't want to sing?" Mavis asked.

"The central police station, finger-printing, calling parents, court appearance, sentencing, punishment, criminal record, rejection by decent society, lives ruined. Feel like singing?" Officer Pup asked.

"Love to sing," Mavis said.

"Good. Go see Hugo Frizzbender. He'll give you your parts and tell you what to do."

"Hugo Frizzbender?"

"Oh, that's right. You know him, I believe. Well, he is the stage manager, and is also playing the Pirate King in this production. There he is, over there, with the eye patch and the cutlass."

LIX.

Hugo Frizzbender wasn't the only person we knew at the Pokooksie Overweight Gilbert and Sullivan Society. There was old Shlermie! It turned out Shlermie was directing that production, and was also playing the role of Major-General Stanley. (Shlermie was one of those who would have to wear a fat-costume when the show was put on before the public.)

We got to hear Shlermie rehearse his big number:

'I am the very model of a modern Major-General,

I've information vegetable, animal, and mineral,

I know the kings of England, and I quote the fights historical,

From Marathon to Waterloo, in order categorical;

I'm very well acquainted too with matters mathematical,

I understand equations, both the simple
and quadratical,

About binomial theorem I'm teeming
with a lot o'news –

With many cheerful facts about the
square of the hypotenuse.'

It went on for about five more stanzas
like that, and Shlermie got through it fast
and perfectly, and it seemed that he
never took a breath. We already admired
old Shlermie, but now we were more im-
pressed than ever.

Our own parts were a lot easier and
consisted of singing things like, "Ta-ran-
ta-ra! Ta-ran-ta-ra!" over and over, which
was kind of fun, actually. And we got to
tiptoe around, dance, and do leaps.

Acting is more fun than striking blows
at the evils of society.

It was also really nice to be with a

group of people where we weren't the only fat ones.

When the meeting and rehearsing was over, Officer Pup said to us, "You'll be here tomorrow night?"

"Or you'll throw us in jail, right?"

"That's right," Officer Pup said. "Though it would give me no pleasure, for . . .

When constabulary duty's to be done

To be done,

The policeman's lot is not a happy one."

LX.

I have to say, Officer Pup knew his business. Twenty-four hours after being arrested and frightened to death, and two hours after discovering the magic of the theater, we were no longer a threat to normal society.

We spent all our time learning lines, practicing singing, learning about making costumes and building sets, and listening to tapes and looking at videos of the great English Gilbert and Sullivan performers.

Of course, the fact that most of the members of the Pokooksie Overweight Gilbert and Sullivan Society were fat, and all of them were talented, was completely cool. There were a few other kids, but we were the youngest. Everybody took care of us and taught us things.

We were going to present *The Pirates of Penzance* to the general public soon, and everybody was working hard to get it ready.

The summer was going way, way too fast.

LXI.

"**Miss Mavis,** I must remind you that your parents will be returning from Africa on Tuesday," old Shlermie said. Even though Shlermie told us what to do at rehearsals, he still called Mavis "Miss Mavis" around the house.

Sylvia and I looked at each other. That meant Camp Noo Yoo would be finishing up for the summer, the survivors would be getting on buses, and Dick Tator would finally realize he didn't know where we were and call our parents. It also meant that our summer hiding out at Mavis's house and being social-reform activists and actors was ending. Only we were going to keep being actors.

LXII.

Old Shlermie prepared a special meal for our last night at Mavis's house, after which we all went to rehearsal, and then came back for dessert, which was double chocolate cake and mint tea – both better than they served at the bookstore.

Early in the morning, Sylvia and I turned up at our house, dragging our duffel bags.

"Look! They're here!" our mother shouted. "What are you doing home already? We were going to meet your bus in the afternoon."

"We took an early bus," I said. Which was true – I just neglected to mention it had been several weeks early.

"You kids look great!" our father said. "You're glowing with health! Aren't you glad we convinced you to go to Noo Yoo?"

"We'll discuss it later," Sylvia said. "How did you and Mom do with the dieting while we were gone?"

"We'll discuss it later," our mother said. "But we've got a coming-home surprise for you. Tell them, dear."

"We're going out to dinner," my father said. "Someplace really nice - and then, we're all going to the theater. Have you ever heard of the Pokooksie Overweight Gilbert and Sullivan Society?"

"As a matter of fact, we have," I said.

"Well, they're putting on a performance of *The Pirates of Penzance,* and we're taking you tonight. That's the surprise. What do you think of it?"

"Pretty good," we said. "We may have a surprise for you, too."

"It's good to have you home, kids," our parents said.

"It's good to be home," we said.